Bold Billy's Space Adventure

Brett Ogley

ISBN 979-8-46-020300-0

In Bold Billy's garden stood a craft, tall, red and silver was its shaft.

In this craft Bold Billy
planned to go to space where
comets orbit and stars glow.

With the most magical speed
Bold Billy set off high until
gone was the moon and all
the sky.

Then it appeared for Bold Billy to see, planet Mars, and oh so very, very clearly!

Orange and red like sand and fire, its rocky expanse so easy to admire.

On Bold Billy went further
still to Jupiter next which was
sure to be a thrill.

Its big red spot such a curiosity, in fact a storm of great ferocity.

Saturn followed and took
Bold Billy by surprise,
although not quite Jupiter's
same humongous size.

Its many moons and icy rings truly were such amazing things.

Then came Uranus in plain view, windy and cold but beautiful too.

Neptune next with its dazzling hue, a fantastic shade of brilliant blue.

But morning was dawning, and Bold Billy knew, if not home soon all havoc would ensue.

So off Bold Billy set with his magic fuel, destined for planet Earth – our fragile jewel.

All the way home Bold Billy was full of glee because next time he would see Venus and maybe Mercury…!

If your little one loved this story then why not leave its author some glory? A five-star review goes a long way, so I'd be truly grateful if you post one today.

Bold Billy's Space Adventure is also available as a colouring book.

www.boldbilly.com